Trains
Byron Barton

Thomas Y. Crowell   New York

Copyright © 1986 by Byron Barton. Printed in Italy. All rights reserved. First Edition
Library of Congress Cataloging-in-Publication Data   Barton, Byron. Trains. Summary: Brief text and
illustrations present a variety of trains and what they do.   1. Railroads—Juvenile literature.
[1. Railroads—Trains] I. Title.   TF148.B27 1986   385'.37   [E]   85-47898   ISBN 0-694-00061-2
690-04534-4 (lib. bdg.)

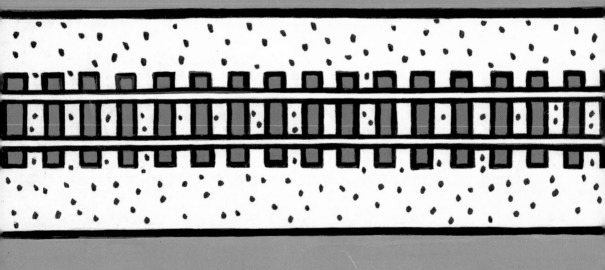

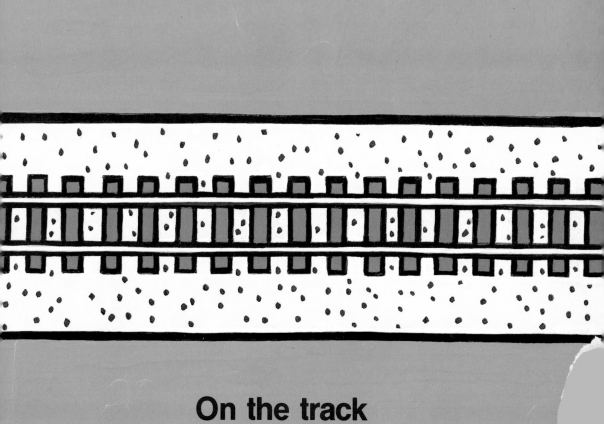

On the track

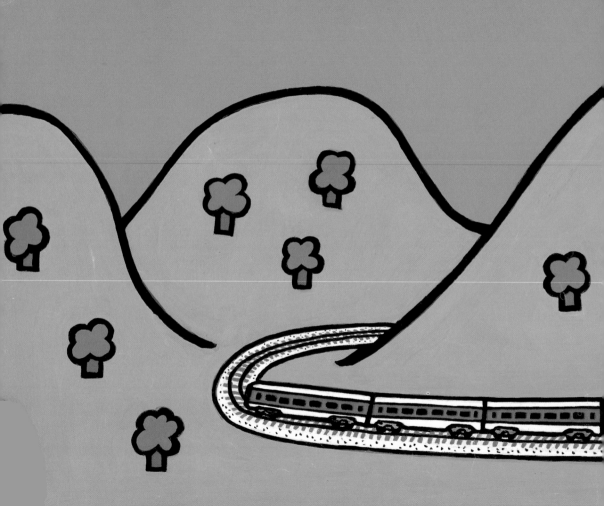

the trains are running.

Here is a train

with people inside.

There goes a freight train

loaded with freight.

Here are the freight cars.

The caboose is last.

Here is a steam engine

puffing smoke.

There is an electric train.

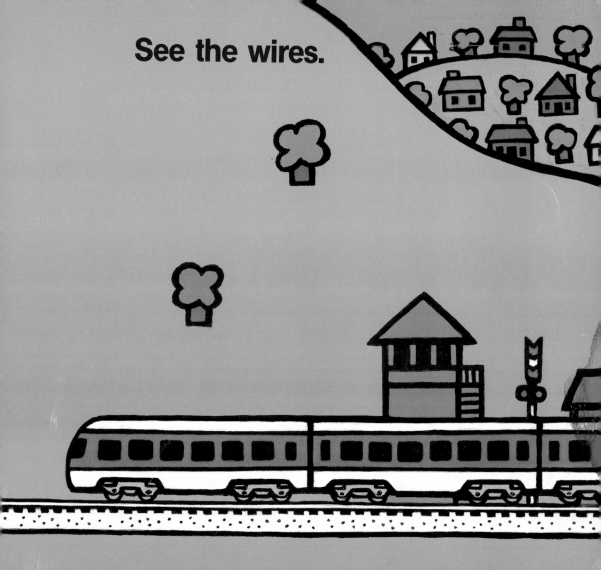

See the wires.

Here are some workers

fixing the track.

Here is the engineer

driving at night.

Here are the passengers

sound asleep.

Here is a railroad crossing.

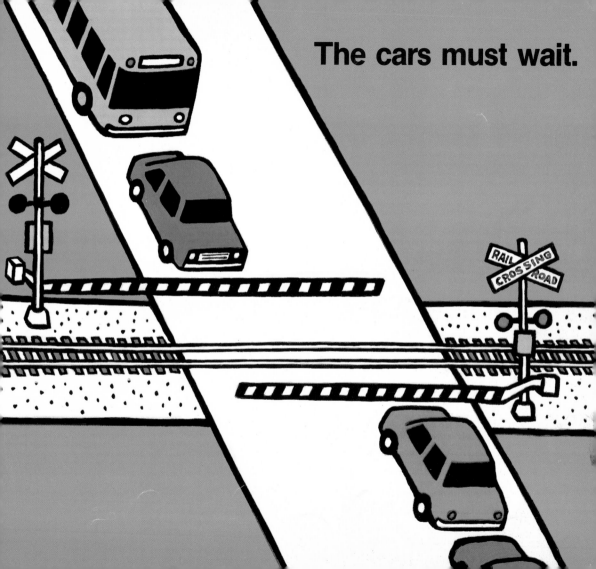

The cars must wait.

Here is a town.

The train passes by.

Here is a train station.

The train stops here.

Here are the people

getting on and off.

Here is the conductor calling,

There goes the train speeding away.